THE CHRISTIAN CRUSADER ™

BY JOHN CELESTRI

THE CHRISTIAN CRUSADER ADVENTURE ALBUM SERIES

BOOK I
THE QUEST BEGINS

BOOK II
WEB OF LIES...CHAINS OF SIN

BOOK III
PLAGUE OF EVIL

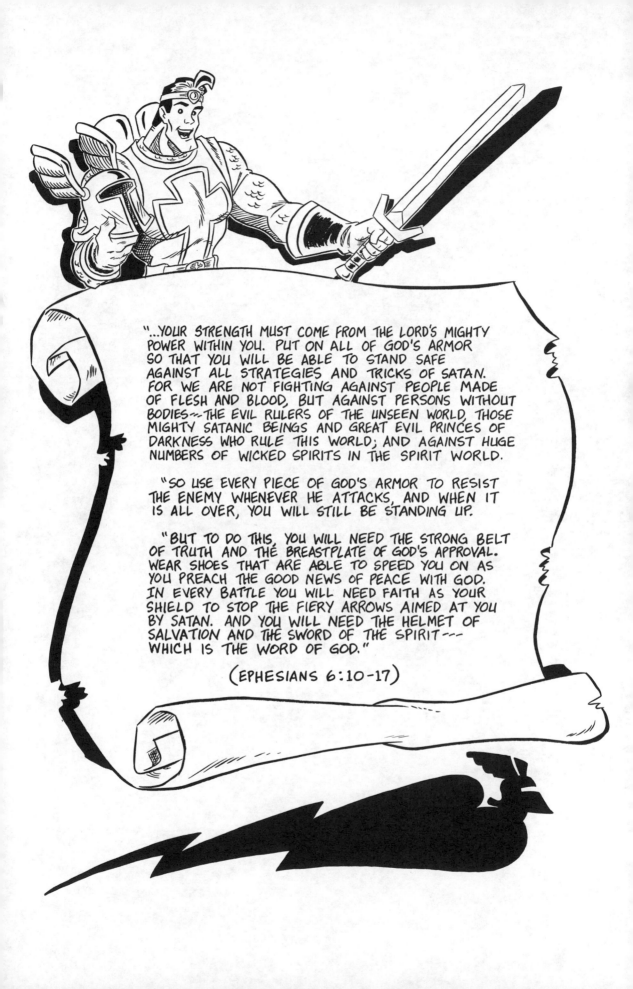

"...YOUR STRENGTH MUST COME FROM THE LORD'S MIGHTY POWER WITHIN YOU. PUT ON ALL OF GOD'S ARMOR SO THAT YOU WILL BE ABLE TO STAND SAFE AGAINST ALL STRATEGIES AND TRICKS OF SATAN. FOR WE ARE NOT FIGHTING AGAINST PEOPLE MADE OF FLESH AND BLOOD, BUT AGAINST PERSONS WITHOUT BODIES---THE EVIL RULERS OF THE UNSEEN WORLD, THOSE MIGHTY SATANIC BEINGS AND GREAT EVIL PRINCES OF DARKNESS WHO RULE THIS WORLD; AND AGAINST HUGE NUMBERS OF WICKED SPIRITS IN THE SPIRIT WORLD.

"SO USE EVERY PIECE OF GOD'S ARMOR TO RESIST THE ENEMY WHENEVER HE ATTACKS, AND WHEN IT IS ALL OVER, YOU WILL STILL BE STANDING UP.

"BUT TO DO THIS, YOU WILL NEED THE STRONG BELT OF TRUTH AND THE BREASTPLATE OF GOD'S APPROVAL. WEAR SHOES THAT ARE ABLE TO SPEED YOU ON AS YOU PREACH THE GOOD NEWS OF PEACE WITH GOD. IN EVERY BATTLE YOU WILL NEED FAITH AS YOUR SHIELD TO STOP THE FIERY ARROWS AIMED AT YOU BY SATAN. AND YOU WILL NEED THE HELMET OF SALVATION AND THE SWORD OF THE SPIRIT--- WHICH IS THE WORD OF GOD."

(EPHESIANS 6:10-17)

KNIGHTS of CHRIST

CODE OF CONDUCT

I

KEEP GOD'S COMMANDMENTS.

II

DON'T ABUSE YOUR BODY---
DON'T USE COCAINE OR
ANY STREET DRUGS.

III

NEVER TAKE ADVANTAGE OF OTHERS.

IV

HELP THE LESS FORTUNATE.

V

ASK JESUS CHRIST TO EMPOWER YOU
TO DO YOUR BEST EVERY DAY.

Front and back covers produced in conjunction
with ZENDER & ASSOCIATES, CINCINNATI, OHIO

Published by CC COMICS, PO Box 542, Loveland, Ohio 45140.

First Edition: September 1993

ISBN 0-9634183-2-7

Printed in the United States of America

ON THE OPPOSITE END OF THE UNIVERSE --- AT THE POINT FARTHEST FROM THE PLANET EARTH --- EXISTS A WORLD NAMED **THREA!**

THE GOOD NEWS OF JESUS CHRIST HAS BEEN SOWN THERE, BUT IT IS A WORLD OF ROCKY SOIL AND THERE ARE VERY FEW FERTILE SPOTS FOR **GOD'S SEED (WORD)** TO GROW! *

* MATTHEW 13:3

SATAN'S AGENT, **ZA-TIN THE UNHOLY ONE,** HAS CONQUERED ALL OF **THREA....** EVERYTHING IS UNDER THE DOMINATION OF HIS IRON FIST --- **EXCEPT FOR ONE PERSON...**

THE CHRISTIAN CRUSADER!

SIR DAVID IS **THE LAST KNIGHT OF CHRIST,** AND AS THE CHRISTIAN CRUSADER HE DEDICATES HIS LIFE TO SPREADING **THE WORD OF GOD...**

... AND BATTLES THE FORCES OF EVIL AS **A CHAMPION OF OUR LORD JESUS CHRIST!**

21

31

IF YOU WANT CHRISTIAN COMIC BOOKS,
YOU NEED THE NEWEST EDITION OF THE

CHRISTIAN COMICS CATALOG

FOR THE *BEST* IN NEW AND VINTAGE
COMICS-- FOR *ALL* AGE GROUPS!
JUST TEAR OUT THIS CARD, TYPE OR PRINT
YOUR INFORMATION BELOW, ATTACH A
FIRST-CLASS POSTAGE STAMP, AND
MAIL IT IN *TODAY* FOR YOUR *FREE* COPY!

NAME: _____

ADDRESS: _____

CITY: _____

STATE: _____ ZIP:_____

. . .OR YOU CAN *FAX* THIS INFORMATION TO:
(505) 260-0190

FIRST CLASS MAIL

CHRISTIAN COMICS CATALOG ™
C/O THE NATE BUTLER STUDIO, INC.
P.O. BOX 27470 - DEPT. CJ
ALBUQUERQUE, NM 87125-7470

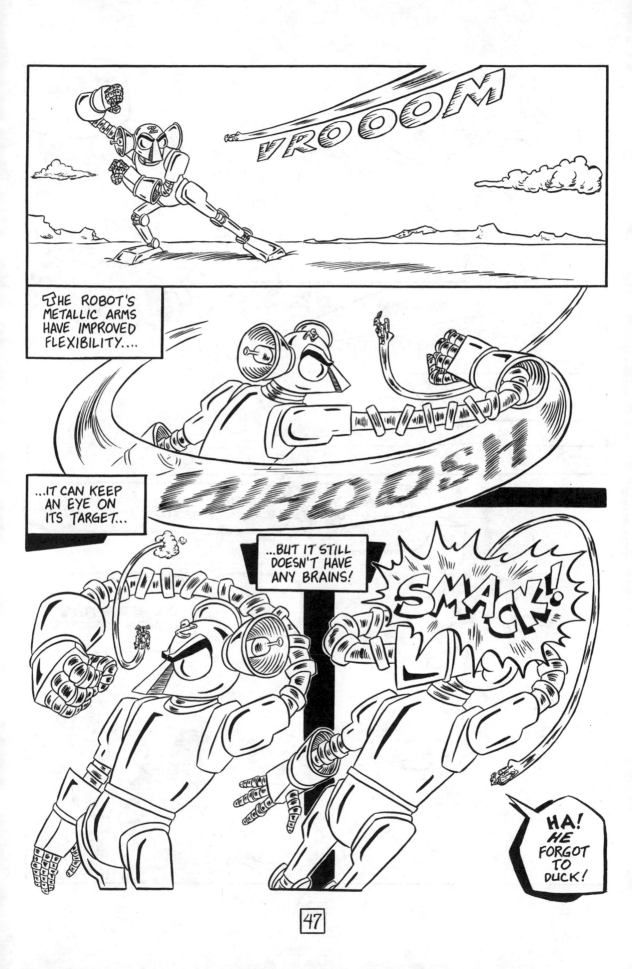

THAT'LL KEEP HIM OCCUPIED FOR A WHILE!

FWOOOSH!

SIR DAVID CATCHES UP TO THE NEW CHRISTIANS!

THAT ROBOT CAN DO A LOT OF NEW TRICKS!

ZA-TIN'S TEMPTATION-WEAPONS LAB MUST BE HARD AT WORK!

I KNOW~~~

~~~I USED TO BE ONE OF ZA-TIN'S WEAPONS ENGINEERS!

*SEE BOOK I: "THE QUEST BEGINS"

61

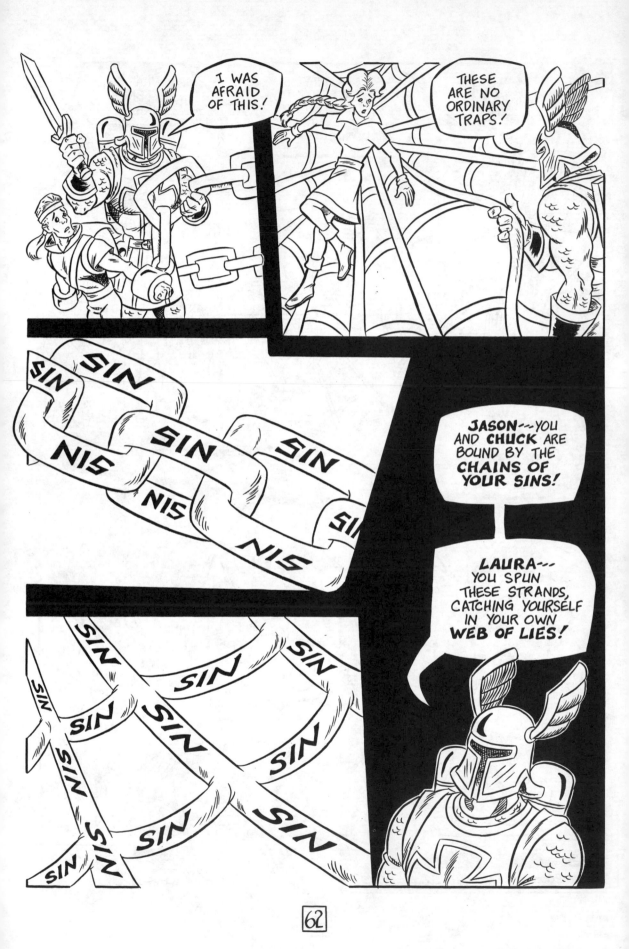